# THE EXPLORERS

Jane Keys

M

Illustrated by Leigh Murrell

Mum says we are having visitors to lunch.
Bear and I must be very good.

For James Leslie and
Peter Emmanuel

First published 1989 by
THE MACMILLAN COMPANY OF AUSTRALIA PTY LTD
107 Moray Street, South Melbourne 3205
6 Clarke Street, Crows Nest 2065

Associated companies and representatives throughout the world

Keys, Jane, 1956–  .
  The explorers.

  ISBN 0 333 50230 2.

  I. Murrell, Leigh. II. Title.

A823′.3

Set in Baskerville by Savage Type Pty Ltd, Brisbane
Colour Separations by Hong Kong Graphic Arts Ltd
Printed in Hong Kong

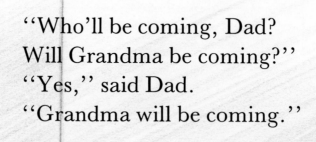

"Who'll be coming, Dad?
Will Grandma be coming?"
"Yes," said Dad.
"Grandma will be coming."

''Good, I can take Grandma exploring.''

When I go to Grandma's, we explore the plains together.

"Who'll be coming, Dad?
Will Grandpa James be coming?"
"Yes," said Dad.
"Grandpa James will be coming."

"Good, I can take Grandpa James exploring."

When I go to Grandpa James', we explore the jungle together.

"Who'll be coming, Mum?
Will Grandpa Peter be coming?"
"Yes," said Mum.
"Grandpa Peter will be coming."

''Good, I can take Grandpa Peter exploring.''

When I go to Grandpa Peter's, we explore space together.

"Who'll be coming, Dad?
Will Aunty Irene be coming?"
"Yes," said Dad.
"Aunty Irene will be coming."

"Good, I can take Aunty Irene exploring."

When I go to Aunty Irene's, we explore the sea together.

"Who'll be coming, Mum?
Will Ivy be coming?"
"Yes," said Mum.
"Ivy will be coming."

"Good, I can take Ivy exploring."

When I go to Ivy's, we explore caves together.

"Here they come."

"Hello, Grandma.
Hello, Grandpa James.
Can we go exploring now?"
"After lunch, darling."

"Can we blast off into space, Grandpa Peter?"
"After lunch, Sara."

"Uncle Jack! No one told me you were coming."
"I've come to take you exploring."

"Now I know why the rest of you wouldn't come exploring with me."

"Where will we go exploring today, Uncle Jack?"
"Let's just wait and see."